Lost

A Chosen Novella

Andrea Lynn Ford

CREATIVE FLIGHT PUBLISHING
Newark

Creative Flight Publishing

ISBN-13: 978-0-9890033-7-7

Printed in the United States of America

Book Two

If I were loved, as I desire to be, what is there in the great sphere of the earth, and rangc of evil between death and birth, that I should fear, - if I were loved by thee?

Alfred Tennyson

Trust

So this is Hell, I thought. Somehow my lacking knowledge had me picturing spitfire, murky skies, and insufferable heat. You know, the generic crap spewed to the masses in order to scare them into doing the right thing. I have to hand it to Lucifer though, this place was nice.

We arrived in what appeared to be a lobby of an office building. Well-dressed men and women were entering and exiting through the tall glass doors to our left. The women's heels clicked across the elegant marble floors, making beautiful music with the rhythm.

My eyes were drawn to the priceless artwork that hung in gold frames on the walls. I found that the entire room had old world sophistication. It was the kind of place you would expect Humphrey Bogart to come walking out.

There was a large desk in the middle that had a sweet looking blond in glasses seated behind it. She appeared to be working on a computer. Who knew Hell had Wi-Fi? My escorts led the way through the lobby to the desk.

I tried my best not to fidget, but it was painfully clear that I did not belong. The blond peaked around the motley crew. She slid her glasses down to the tip of her nose in order to appraise me.

"Well, what do we have here, Matthias?" She asked speculatively.

His name is Matthias... Good to know. This woman, I'm sure, was asking questions that were above her pay grade.

"I have strict orders to bring her to Lucifer, Greta," he responded in a flirtatious manner. She was not impressed. Greta simply nodded her acceptance of his orders, and began checking her computer for what I believe was authorization.

I buried my laughter. W-O-W even in Hell these snatchers were disgusting to women. After a few moments of checking the computer, Greta backed away from the screen shocked. Her troubled expression could not be a good sign.

I stepped forward, "Is there a problem?" I asked as calmly as I could manage. "You see, I'm a busy girl, my time is precious. I know that I have a meeting, so could you buzz us through, or hand us a pass? I suggested. "Basically do whatever it is you do to get us moving."

My attitude was meant to be confident, but I'm pretty sure it came across snotty. Matthias was suddenly in my face scowling.

"Have you ever heard of personal space, Matthias? Step off. I'm quite sure Lucifer would not like you upsetting me again. Should you confer with Mac? Oh that's right…" I brushed past him towards the gold trimmed elevator doors.

Matthias was not having it. He reached out and grabbed my arm with such brutality that I was sure to bruise. At that moment, I truly wished I had some sort of Angelic power that could sting his punk ass. Instead, I ripped my arm from his hold, spun around, and met his eyes. His stare was far more impressive, but mine must have held something, for he backed off.

Just then, the elevator door opened. I gathered myself and proceeded to board. Matthias backed away mumbling apologies and bowing before the man in the elevator.

"My humbled apologies, Azazel. Miss, here," Matthias said gesturing to me, "would not heed my warnings. She preceded without me, Sir."

"Stand up you fool," Azazel commanded.

I took that moment to graciously bow my head before speaking. "Azazel darling, it's me, Amitiel. I was on my way to see Lucifer. Perhaps you could escort me? This Matthias of yours, is working on my last nerve, you see." I spoke with great reverence and fortitude, as

Azazel looked like a man of great standing, for Hell anyway.

Azazel admired me curiously. He dismissed my unwanted escorts, and gently ushered me onto the elevator platform.

Viewing this gesture as a great honor, I lowered my eyes and linked my arm with his, accepting his escort gladly.

Hell so far was not a bad place. Perhaps a bit unorganized, and could use better help, but man the digs had promise. Even Azazel here, was nice to look at. He donned a fine suit, gray in color of which I'm almost certain was made of fine Italian silk. His hair was midnight black, cropped nicely above his ears. Only a few stay strands fell near is piercing brown eyes. A girl could do worse, as escorts go.

"It is so nice to see you again, Amitiel," Azazel said kissing my hand politely.

Blushing, I responded, "It is quite a pleasure. I've only recently acquired my memories."

"Sorry to hear," he laughed. "And they call God moral," Azazel mocked.

"Who's to say who is or is not moral? All I know is, I've been dealt a raw deal, and now I must go around and clean up the mess," I retorted using the same mocking tone as he did.

I figured the safest bet was to be on his good side for now. Azazel was charming and held great power in Heaven long ago from what I remember. Who knew what his capabilities were in Hell?

Azazel grinned. "Spoken like a true diplomat."

"I'm afraid these are rough times," I said trying to sound sincere. "Between my fall, and the recent knowledge that I've acquired, I feel things have gotten out of control in my absence."

We had reached the top floor. Still playing my polite girl role perfectly, Azazel continued to lead the way. Once we exited, we began down a long beautiful corridor towards the closed double doors at the end.

"You are quite the gentleman, Azazel. Thank you for escorting me. I may not be vengeful, but Matthias was sure to feel something." I gave a gentle laugh, and batted my eyes keeping the conversation flowing.

Boy did he soak up the flirtatious praise. "You are most welcome, dear Amitiel. Do make sure you ask for me from now on, to avoid using less than hospitable channels in regard to your visits," he bowed before opening the doors for me.

Open the doors he did too. The elegant lobby was nothing compared to the glorious sight before me. It was luxury at its finest. The entire room was encased in tall windows that overlooked what appeared to be an ocean. If I had not known I was in Hell, I would have thought it was Malibu, overlooking the great Pacific.

There was wall-to-wall gold carpet, with white leather sofas arranged in a semi circle. Beautiful roses ornamented the coffee table amidst the seating. In the far corner there was an opulent desk cluttered with stacks and stacks of files. Above the desk was a plaque that read: **I am the Lord your God. You shall not have strange Gods before me.** *How ironic*, I thought.

My appraisal stopped there, as I laid eyes on him. Lucifer sat behind the desk shuffling through papers. His glasses hung low on his angular nose; his blue and red silk striped tie was loosened for comfort. He was unmistakably in charge here. Lucifer's mere presence radiated authority. I felt the urge to curtsey, but resisted.

"Brother, Amitiel has arrived," Azazel said clearing his throat.

Lucifer, who until that moment was clearly unaware of our entrance, stood up, removed his glasses, and straightened his tie. "Please excuse my appearance, Amitiel, for I had not received word of your arrival."

Moving swiftly around the desk, Lucifer stood before Azazel and I, though his eyes never left mine.

"It's good to see you, Lucifer, my brother. Upon heading home, I stumbled upon Amitiel. Matthias was hassling her. I felt it was my duty to bring her to you safely," Azazel stated earnestly.

"You are dismissed with my gratitude, brother," Lucifer replied gesturing for Azazel to exit the room and leave us alone.

Azazel bowed before him, and retreated out the door.

Lucifer clasped his hands together clearly pleased with our privacy, and ushered me towards the sofa. Snapping his fingers, an assistant appeared.

"Can I offer you a drink, or a bite to eat? You must be ravished after your journey."

Until that moment, I actually had not thought about it. All the nerves and such had kept me preoccupied. Once hunger was brought to the forefront of my thoughts, I realized I truly was ravished, as he put it.

"I would love a B.L.T. and an iced cold glass of tea, if it is not too much trouble," I requested politely.

"You are ever my darling, Amitiel. It is no bother. Bring her what she requires," Lucifer barked to his assistant. She disappeared, instantly obeying.

"Thank you for your hospitality. I do recall our friendship with a great fondness."

"I did hear that the fall rendered you mindless, was that incorrect?"

"No. In fact, until recently I had no recollection of my prior life at all. I'm embarrassed to even speak that I was also unaware of being an Angel."

"You were always my favorite, Amitiel. How could you not be? With beauty like yours, you should rule the world," he gushed.

"How sweet of you to say. I accept your kind words gladly," I chuckled.

"It has been too long. Thank you for coming to see me. I realize it must have been awful learning the truth," he stated, referring to my push rather than fall.

"You're welcome, and it most definitely was heart-breaking," I shared, referring to the havoc he had wreaked on earth.

The glint in his deep blue gray eyes told me he caught my inference. The way he held my gaze was beginning to confuse me. He looked at me like I was the sun in his otherwise dark world. Like I was his to behold. It was hard to remain coherent in his presence when he looked at me that way.

Thank goodness my food appeared when it did. Lucifer's assistant's arrival broke the intense moment. She quietly laid out my sandwich and tea before me, and retreated just as silently.

I smiled kindly at him, and began to eat. The B.L.T. looked amazing. I was even brought fresh fruit and potato chips on the side. I had to admit that I still did not see the downside of Hell yet.

By the time I was finished with my lunch, I began to feel more comfortable. I stretched out on the sofa and made myself at home.

"So I'm sure you know by now that my visit isn't purely social," I said broaching the true subject of my trip.

"I assumed, though I wish it were otherwise." His smile faded. "I've missed you. Life does not go on as it should with you absent. It was not only your Buer that was hurt with your fall. I too suffered in your dearth," he confessed.

"You suffered? How so, dear friend?" I was completely blindsided by his confession.

"Does your memory still lack? I was sure at first that you remembered our former tryst. I thought that perhaps you only feigned to hide your true feelings for me. I see now that I am mistaken," Lucifer mourned, calculating his next move. He turned towards me outstretched on the couch, "I loved you, Amitiel. I still do, even with all the chaos that's ensued."

Lucifer genuinely looked serene. My thoughts were far from it. I recalled our relationship quite differently. Did I at one time care for him? Sure, as a friend. Did I once love this man too? Of course I did, but definitely not romantically.

"Chaos indeed. How do you explain yourself, Luc?" I fondly recalled the nickname I had for my once dear friend.

"My how I've longed to hear you call me Luc," he sighed happily. "Would you forgive me if I told you it was to avenge your fall?"

"Vengeance has never been necessary. Though I do not seem to remember the argument that came before my fall, I do trust God enough to have had a purposeful reason behind it."

"Blasphemy!" He yelled, outraged. "That twit of a brother of mine had no right to punish you for my love, or Buers for that matter." He spit the name Buer as if it tasted bad in his mouth. Calming himself, he smoothed out his features and continued, "You were created with perfection in mind. Amitiel, Angel of Truth, your beauty and sensibility are something to be honored. With the free will you were granted, you chose to love. Why should there be a double standard?"

If I were being honest with myself, I would have to admit that the doubt Luc just planted in my head was working. Why should there be a double standard? Even if my love was founded from a loophole in Gods plan, why should that be a punishable crime?

Lucifer watched patiently with a knowing look. He had me. I could not answer his question. Perhaps he meant for it to be that way. The smile on his face, and the loving look in his beautiful eyes never did cease. I had to keep from looking at him if I was to get to my point. I had to remember why I was here.

I felt honesty from Lucifer, but was that a ruse? I could not be sure. Sadly my friend had changed.

"You believe that my fall was to punish you rather than me, or Buer? It was my love that ruined everything?" I suddenly was overcome with emotion.

Lucifer's face became distraught from witnessing my emotions. He quickly lifted from his seat, and sat beside me to lend his shoulder for comfort. I leaned into his broad chest and cried, heaving deep sobs. I cried from exhaustion, I cried from confusion, and I cried for the loss I felt when I looked into Luc's eyes. My dear friend was lost.

It takes a strong man not to run from tears. Lucifer caressed my back while I cried for what seemed like hours. Time is not measured here. Time – That made me realize the importance of urgency. Bow was wounded after all, and he needed me. I had to keep it together for him.

"Thank you," I mumbled softly composing myself once again. "I realize there is much to discuss between us, however, I need to get back to Buer. He is wounded, you know."

"Buer is in good hands, love. Temperance has him now." When my expression was puzzled, he tapped his forehead in explanation. Of course he would be privy to all that goes on.

"That may be true, but I still must get down to business. I am here for the lost souls you've acquired." Sensing his next move, I raised my hand in pause and added, "Let me clarify, I'm here for the Fallen."

"I see. I suppose arrangements could be made. You do know they are here of their own free will though. I cannot force them to go, as God seems to think He can," he sneered.

I chose to ignore his comment about God. "A man of your stature and power surly could influence a decision or two." I tried using Temperance's suggestion of flattery.

"Why do you want them?" He wondered aloud.

"Angels weren't meant to roam outside of Heaven. You know that." I tilted my head and probed into his eyes for understanding. "I need to redeem them. I must send them back."

"Send them back, you say? Even if you are not allowed back yourself?" He pushed incredulously.

"Yes, even if I am not allowed entrance. It is my destiny, Luc. I need to fulfill it. They are hurting. The Fallen need *you* to help in their salvation."

"Why would I influence the masses to retreat to Heaven, when I despise my brother for his holy arrogance and the Hell he created the day you fell?"

Leaning back into the sofa, and away from his sculpted form, I regrouped. Lucifer posed good questions. *Why should he?*

"With all do respect, Luc, *you* created Hell. While I agree the pain God caused you is unforgivable, I won't stand for the others to be damned with your despair."

Lucifer fell back against the cushion as if I had slapped him. In that moment, his face fell and formed into a hard mask. The same mask, I am sure, he has worn for years in my absence. His glare became hostile.

It was now my turn to back away. The phrase, 'if looks could kill' came to mind. As hurt as I was by Lucifer's mood swing, I realized that what I said came across as insensitive. I had to remind myself that I was not just Ami the girl. I had to think like Amitiel the Angel. It was not my place to judge.

I scooted closer to his side and rested my hand on his knee in comfort. I half expected him to pull away, but he melted at my touch.

"I'm sorry. It is not my place to judge, Luc. I know you're hurting," I said trying to smooth things out.

"Hurt has no place in my black heart. Only your love can rectify this bitter old man."

"Be that as it may, I feel your heart is not as black as you think it is. You, my dear Luc, are better than this. May I please redeem the Fallen? I came to you for your permission."

Lucifer rose from where we sat, and began to pace the row of windows. The sky outside had turned an awful gray. The same way the sky on Earth turns gray before a storm. I was unaware of how Hell worked. This creation of Lucifer's seemed to bend to his will.

His pacing continued for quite some time. I began to feel sleepy. This had been a long day. I interrupted his reverie, "I find myself tired, Luc. You seem to have thoughts you're not sharing with me. Perchance, could I beg upon your further hospitality for a place to stay the night?"

Lucifer was caught off guard. "Where are my manners? Of course you may. Nothing would please me more. My love, my home is your home," he said clapping his hands together, an action that made his office disappear, and a new surrounding rise around us.

Well, that was cool! Luc and I now seemed to be at his house on the beach, possibly the same beach that his tower office overlooked. I was standing in the middle of his living room now, looking out towards the angry waves. Lucifer was opening all the doors that led to the sand, letting in the cool air. The gusts of wind tossed the gold colored curtains, bringing forward a flash of memory.

"Impressive how much you remember," I said assessing the place. Oddly, his home looked like my house in Heaven.

"This old thing?" He mocked.

I could tell he was pleased with the circumstances. I watched him re-loosen. and take off his tie. He unbuttoned the first few buttons of his collared shirt exposing his chest, and then unbuttoned his cuffs rolling up his sleeves to showcase his muscular forearms. He watched me, as I watched him mesmerized. Luc kicked off his shoes before he spoke up.

"Please make yourself at home, love. I think you'll find everything to your liking. I did my best to replicate your home from long ago."

I knew it looked familiar. How thoughtful.

"Once again, you've outdone yourself." I paused rubbing my temples. "It has been an extremely long day, and I fear my eyes will close soon. Will you show me to my room, or is it still the same?" I asked with a smirk.

Luc smiled. "It is the same. I am not worthy of sleeping where you've slept," he said with a slight bow of his head.

Modesty. Perhaps there was hope for my lost friend yet. "Well then, goodnight, dear Luc."

"Goodnight, love."

Strength

It was hard to tear myself from Luc last night. I kept hoping that I would get through to him, and resurrect the graceful Angel I once knew. I would get a glimpse of a forgotten conversation now and then. I could barely remember the 'us' he referred to. I wanted just a little glimpse of the girl he loved and missed. I could not be sure if I was still that girl. Bow held my heart. He was my soul's mate, and that, I was one hundred percent sure of.

The beach house Luc created was enchanted. It must have taken him a great deal of time to hammer out all of the little details. For instance, the den walls were lined with all of my favorite books and poetry just as I left it long ago. My large oil painting of peonies still hung in the formal living room. I hated the fact that I loved it all just as much today, as I did then. I found myself wanting to stay.

I headed to the kitchen slowly. I took my time to admire all of the intimate touches everywhere. I caressed the walnut banister as I descended the stairs, pleased to find an opulent glass vase on a credenza filled with peonies at the base of that staircase. I could feel the happiness I once felt here. It made me sad to think of how he lived in the past. Sorrow gripped my insides at the thought of the pain it must cause him.

"Good morning," I greeted Luc who stood by the stove cooking.

"As to you, Amitiel. How was your night? Did you sleep well?" He asked looking up at me from the eggs he was preparing.

I couldn't help but giggle. He was wearing a pink apron over his navy blue pinstripe suit. "Some more of my memories have been returning – My pink apron for instance…"

Luc strutted up and down the expanse of the kitchen using his best model face. "I am nothing if not thorough," he commented with a fluff of the apron.

"That indeed. I must be going though. I'm afraid your snatchers left a bit of a mess for me on Earth. Bow needs me."

"That he does," Luc admitted full of regret. "I have never stopped loving you, Amitiel." Luc set the pan on the waiting trivet. "I am beginning to understand that I might be fighting fate trying to keep you from Bow with my walk down memory lane," he confessed gesturing to the surroundings.

Reaching for his hands, I tried to explain, "Luc, I do love you, but it is Buer who holds my whole heart. You and I were once great friends, but I am not your soul's mate."

"I know."

"I must heal Buer, Luc. I am not whole without him. It will hurt *me*, to hurt him. Do you understand?"

"Yes. I will concede to your exit from my paradise," he said darkly. "However, I will not interfere with the Fallen. They are here of their own free will. I will tell them of your coming, and tell them where to find you if they choose, but that is as far as I go."

"That is all I am asking, Luc." I caressed his cheek. He leaned his face into it, enjoying the moment.

Pulling away from my touch, Luc grabbed on to my shoulders to look me in the face straight on. His gentle blue-gray eyes were filled with ancient sadness. "By the powers vested in me, by well… *me*, I grant you your exit. Return to me at will, Amitiel, for I will never stop loving you," he concluded. Lucifer then touched my forehead closing the beautiful underworld around me.

†

I would compare my exit from Hell to the downward spiral one feels from a roller coaster. The quick motion itself left my stomach in another dimension, literally.

It took me a few moments to gather myself before I attempted to open my eyes and figure out where Luc dumped me. I just hoped no one happened upon me before I gathered my bearings. Slowly the earth below me stopped moving, and I sat up. Opening my eyes, I immediately knew where I was; the rooftop garden.

I felt terrible. I wanted a hot shower and fresh clothes badly, but I was not steady enough to move yet. My eyes drifted closed. I took a few deep breaths, and called to Bow telepathically. I expected him to come, or at the very least a response, but it was clear after a while that I would receive no such thing. He must be far worse than I had expected. I had to forget the shower and find him.

I mustered up every bit of strength I had. Mentally I kicked myself for not eating breakfast with Luc before I returned. I stood up. The ground wavered for a moment before staying still. I realized that was the best I was going to get, so I took off full speed for the elevator.

Temperance must know where he is, or have some sort of information for me. She was still my Guardian Angel after all. I punched the third floor button as soon as I was in the elevator. My nerves were on edge. I had been in Hell for what felt like one day and night, but I was increasingly aware that the Earth did not stand still in my absence.

I knew I was in trouble the moment I stepped off the elevator on to the once familiar third floor. The stares I received were a range from shock to disbelief. God only knew what I looked like. I hadn't had time to check a mirror. Ignoring everything and everyone, I rushed into Temperance's office.

"Temperance," I called exhausted. I crumbled to the floor the moment I shut the door firmly behind me.

Temperance spun around in her chair and practically flew to my side the instant our eyes met.

"Amitiel," she sighed in relief. "I began to fear the worst. It has been months," she scolded. "What have you been doing?"

"I had no control over the time. I barely spent one night in Hell. I can't believe that it has been that long."

"It has. Things are tense here, Amitiel. Buer is injured badly, I got to him as soon as I could, believe me. There is only so much a Guardian can do."

"I feared that," I sighed exasperated. "I need to go to him. Where is he?" I asked trying to stand.

"Safe. Sit back down. First you must rest. Please tell me, did you meet with Lucifer, how did your journey go?"

"I did," I began, as I gathered myself enough to make it to the sofa. "The plan worked. I met with him fairly quick. There were a few bumps along the way," I said remembering Matthias and Greta. "Azazel found me, and led me to him."

Temperance brought me a bottle of cold water and a blanket. I must look worse than I feared.

"Please continue," she prodded.

"Well, Luc and I go way back of course, but he admitted to loving me. He's created this reality in Hell that rivals the veracity of Heaven. Temperance, he even duplicated my home, and my things…" I took a deep swig of water. I needed the refreshment.

"Lucifer was a great love of yours long ago. I'm not surprised you remember him fondly."

"We spoke about the chaos he's creating. It took all of my strength to leave the underworld and return. He posed so many valid points. Luc feels God punished him for loving me, by sending me away," I confessed with a deep ache in my heart. "I'm responsible for it all, Temperance. Luc created Hell to save himself from the sorrow he felt in my wake."

Temperance put her arm around me drawing me closer to her on the couch. "You cannot blame yourself for the decisions of others."

"I feel responsible. It is so hard not to feel like 'Ami, the overwhelmed seventeen year old nut-ball.' I constantly have to remind myself that this is all bigger than me, that I am, Amitiel the Angel of Truth, the key to salvation," I said laughing at how ridiculous it all sounded.

"You're eighteen," Temperance reminded me with a sweet smile.

"That's right, I am. H-A!"

"Are you well enough to go now?" Temperance asked.

"I think so. I know he needs me. In the obstacle of everything, he never wavered from my side," I said in awed gratitude.

†

We arrived at Bow's loft less than a half hour later. My feet were not moving as fast as I wanted them to go, so I ushered my wings and flew. I didn't care who saw me at that moment. The only thing on my mind was my mate, my love, Bow.

Once in the door, I rushed to his side on the bed. He looked terrible. Months after the fact, and he was still covered in bloody bandages.

I turned to Temperance, "You said I had been gone for months, why is he still bloody?" I questioned furious.

"Angels are quite different from humans, Amitiel. We do not heal without help. You know this. Our kind was never meant to battle.

Angels are to be peaceful beings." Temperance was respectfully sympathetic.

My hands flustered over his ravaged body helpless. I was still grasping the bandage on his head when he woke. Right away his eyes found mine. His aura glowed pink; expressing the love he felt when he looked at me. My heart sank.

"Ami, God it is good to see your face," he whispered closing his eyes releasing a tear. "I was not sure you'd return, love."

"Bow, you must be in pain. I'm so sorry I left you the way I did. I would have returned to you sooner had I known how. What can I do for you?"

"Stop worrying about me. You are the one who looks like Hell," he attempted to joke, but the spasms from the laughter shook him causing great pain. He winced.

I hopelessly pat and caressed his wounds. Let's face it, I barely understood my powers at this point. Even if I could heal him, I wouldn't know how. Temperance had said that Guardians could not heal, but she didn't qualify whether or not she knew how an Angel was to heal.

With a plan forming in my head, I turned to Temperance who was anxiously biting her manicured nails.

"Tell me how to heal him!" I screamed in command.

Right away she was on the defense, "Even if I knew, Amitiel, you are not in any condition to exert yourself like that. Healing takes the strength from you, and transfers it to the wounded."

"Temperance, I will not take no for an answer." I tried to express my urgency through gritted teeth.

"You must rest first," she said trying to persuade.

"I will not rest until he is on the mend. So either you help me, or I try to figure it out on my own." I was running out of steam. Fighting with Temperance was pointless.

"There is much you do not understand. We have limitations."

I sent a murderous glare in her direction.

"I can tell, however, from your expression that you will not listen, so you have left me no choice other than helping you."

"Good. How do I begin?"

"Alright, let me see… Close your eyes, and take deep breaths. Clear your mind, and find Bow in your thoughts — Have you gotten that far yet?"

"Yes."

"Good, now rest your hands above his chest. Be careful not to press them down, just simply hover."

I did as she instructed.

"Very well, Ami. Now I want you to envision peace, and a healing green light, similar to an aura, surrounding him. This next part is going to be very important," she stressed.

Temperance came to my side where I was kneeling on the floor beside Bow's bed. She rested her hands on my shoulders. I could feel her transferring her strength to me. At first I wanted to back away. I did not want Temperance leaving herself vulnerable for me. I settled on the fact that it was her duty as my Guardian.

"Now you must strip yourself of energy, and send it through your heart, down your hands, and let it exit through your palms. Envision the green light mending all of his wounds, drying all of the blood, and fading all of his bruises. Envision a healthy form beneath your fingertips. Remember to take deeps breaths throughout this entire process," Temperance guided.

I did as she told. I could feel my energy leaving, as if I pulled an all-nighter. I was draining myself in order to save him. My hands felt hot. The energy was warming them as it transferred. I broke out in a cold sweat. The exertion I was feeling felt wrong. The entire process was a fight against nature. Everything in me told me to, 'save myself'. I could not listen to it, though. I loved Bow, and he needed healing.

I knew it was working. I could feel him growing stronger. His emotions were clear. Bow was yelling at me telepathically to stop, but I just kept sending back my refusals. I would not stop halfway through. I would heal him completely. I was determined.

Bow was nearly healed when I decided to open my eyes. When I did, the scene was quite a spectacle. Temperance was anxiously pacing the length of his loft, biting her perfect nails down to nothing. Bow lay motionless beneath my fingertips, his aura glowing a magnificent forest green. I could literally see the energy traveling over his body sewing the wounds shut. The blood sparkled and seeped back into his once torn flesh. The bruises that covered his body were the only evidence left of the peril he faced. Slowly they began to fade, leaving his form perfect and renewed.

At the exact moment his health was restored, three things rapidly transpired. I felt the deep sensation something was terribly wrong, followed by the drastic dimming of my life force. Within seconds the room around me fell from my sight as my soul slipped away from my body. I didn't even have the time to utter 'I love you' to Bow, before the Earth no longer held me in focus.

"No!" Cried Bow helplessly, as he leapt from the bed to catch me before my head hit the floor.

Temperance swiftly moved to his side, an expression of horror distorted her lovely features. She wrapped my lifeless body in a hug and lowered her head in grief.

"I'm here!" I screamed from the corner of the room, but it was no use. They could not see me, or hear my cries any longer.

Gone

It took me a full five minutes of endless screaming, and my voice to crack, before I understood that they could not hear me. It then took me another twenty to calm down enough to observe what was going on in the loft.

Temperance tore Bow from my body and forced him to leave.

"It's for your own good," she urged in hushed tones. "You cannot be present for this." Temperance was stern, but appropriately sympathetic to the situation.

Between sobs Bow answered, "How am I to forgive myself for this? She's gone and it's all my fault!" The pain from the loss had him doubled over.

Halfway out the door he looked back to where my body was crumpled on the floor. It looked as though he would run back to my side, but Temperance gently nudged him, and told him he could return in an hour.

I looked down at myself. I appeared to be whole, but seeing my broken empty body lying on the floor made me relive the moment my soul escaped. How could Bow feel this was his fault? I would not heed anyone's warnings. I did this. I was too stubborn, as always.

Once Bow was gone, Temperance gathered my lifeless body in her arms, and carried it to the bathroom. She gently removed my dirty tattered white dress that I had been wearing since before my trip to Hell, and drew a bath. Temperance caressed my cheek, "What have you done, my dear?" She whispered to my body.

With all of her strength, she lifted my naked body into the filled tub. Once she had it situated, she collapsed on to the tile floor. Her sobs were deep and gut wrenching. Black streaks of mascara streamed down her pale face. Her once sparkling emerald green eyes were tired and blood-shot.

Wanting deeply to comfort her, I instantly moved to the bathroom. I realized then, that I could move simply by wishing it so. I reached out to touch my Guardian Angel, but I found that my hand moved right through her. I tried and I tried to make contact with her to show her I was still here and okay, but each time the result was the same; Temperance could not see or feel me.

I sat on the tile floor beside the tub, and quietly watched Temperance kneel before it and bathe my still body like a child. Her dress billowed out around her reminding me of a flower. As she leaned forward to scrub my back, the tips of her beautiful red hair dipped in the water making ripples in the otherwise tranquil water.

I could no longer watch up close. I sat in the doorway to the bathroom, and rested my head on my pulled up knees. This out of body experience felt like a terrible dream.

I continued watching Temperance care for my body. Tears streaked down her face in an endless stream. She was humming an Irish lullaby to me almost in a cooing manner. Her love for me was never more apparent than in that moment. Finally she was finished and she drained the water.

I wasn't sure how she planned to get my body out of the tub. I was scared her slender frame couldn't bare my one hundred and twenty pounds of dead weight, but she lifted me with ease. Embarrassed by the sight of my naked body, I blushed. Thank goodness Temperance wrapped a robe around me.

This entire scene was beginning to anger me. I wanted to scream, but what was the point? My throat was already raw. Temperance dried my still body and placed me in a scarlet wrap dress and heels. I paced up and down the hallway watching her powder my motionless face, and blow dry and curl my chocolate brown hair, all the while I was invisible to her.

Anguish tore through me. I ghosted to her side. "Is there no hope then?" I screamed in her ear. I knew she couldn't hear, though a small part wished that if I was loud enough, she would. "Is this it?" I cried out again even louder. "Am I dead?" It felt good to say the words out loud.

When Temperance finished, she laid my clean and beautiful body on the bed. My anger ebbed as I watched her carefully arrange my soft billowy hair around the pillow. She straightened my dress, and folded my hands on my waist. *All I needed was a casket, and the funeral would be complete!* I thought in frustration.

In a final touch, she removed the locket she wore around her neck, and placed it on mine. I couldn't fathom why Temperance did all of this? If this was it and I was dead, why go through the trouble? Temperance touched the locket lovingly. "Sweet Amitiel, you must find your way back to us," she whispered softly to my still body.

While focusing on the locket she placed around my neck, I realized that my body was not lifeless at all. I could clearly see my chest moving as air entered and left. If my body was breathing, then maybe there was hope.

This new bit of information soothed me, but raised more questions than I could answer. First and foremost, if I was not dead, where was I?

†

Bow returned exactly an hour later. His return made me realize that I still had some of my powers despite my current state. I could clearly see the fear in Bows red aura. He rushed to the bed where my sleeping body rested. Temperance sat quietly in the chair by the corner.

"She looks beautiful, thank you," Bow addressed Temperance.

"Yes," she paused to wipe away her tears, "she does."

"If I didn't know better," Bow said caressing my soft still cheek, "I'd think she was just sleeping."

Temperance chuckled quietly and glided to his side. She rested her hand upon mine. "I suppose she is the quintessential sleeping beauty, is she not?"

His mouth slightly curved up at her fairy tale reference. "Indeed, my love is." He bent down and softly kissed my rose colored lips. The spirit me blushed for my shell no longer could.

"I had to try," Bow softly chuckled. His kiss did not wake me.

†

I quickly found out that my spirit self did not need rest as a body required. I spent the night watching Bow instead. He sat somber next to my still form for hours, reading me poetry. It was some of my favorites too. Instantly, I felt abashed. Of course he would read my favorites. Long ago in Heaven we often spent afternoons reading the very same passages.

"Dearest love," he spoke quietly. "Shall I read you the Poem of Dancing?" Chuckling quietly he reminisced. "Do you remember long ago when we first kissed? I do. Heaven was glorious then. You had given me a new meaning for existing." Bow paused and touched my still lips.

"I remember telling you how you had stolen my heart. My sweet Amitiel… you just laughed at me and told me that I could find your love where riptides met ripples. I was bewitched and bemused. I asked you where that was, and you said, "Where chaos finds peace, silly."" Bow sighed, and started reading the poem by Sir John Davies:

"Learn then to dance, you that are princes born, and lawful lords of earthly creatures all; imitate them, and thereof take no scorn, for this new art to them is natural, and imitate the stars celestial. For when pale death your vital twist shall sever, your better parts must dance with them forever."

It was eerie how that stanza fit this setting so beautifully. Bow closed his book around two in the morning, and found rest beside my body.

I watched him sleep. Occasionally he would toss and mumble under his breath. His sleep did not look restful. I worried for him and the guilt he felt. I wanted to hug him and explain everything. Several times I attempted to. No such luck. As with Temperance, my spirit simply passed through him.

When he finally awoke, it was nearly the afternoon. He gently rose from the bed careful not to jostle my sleeping body. As soft as a butterfly's wing he tenderly skimmed his nose across my throat and whispered, "Good morning." It was heartbreaking to watch him love me when I was no longer present.

I had to get down to business, and figure out where the veil exactly was, and what it meant that I now resided here. Watching Bow only distracted me, so I did my best to ignore him. I drifted around his wide-open loft effortlessly deep in thought.

Making a checklist of all the things I knew, I counted them off on my fingers. First, I assume that I'm not dead. My body breathing, in fact, was proof supporting this assumption. Second, I'm clearly not in Heaven or Hell for that matter. I feel lost. Lastly, it was evident that I still had some of my Angelic powers.

I knew I had to figure out exactly where I could travel. I knew thought was the key to this. I also needed to know what I could do in spirit form if I was ever going to find my way back to my body. I decided to start with the easy stuff.

When Bow left for work, I decided to concentrate on moving objects. I had no real reference point, but I saw the movie Ghost once, and the lead character Sam was dead. I remember that he was able to concentrate really hard on something, and move it, so I figured I'd give it a try.

The movie made it look so easy for him. Mentally I tried, and tried again to move the coffee cup Bow left on the table, but it didn't even budge. Completely frustrated, I decided to extend my hands before it and give it a metaphysical shove. The only thing that did was end up manifesting an identical cup in my hands. *Holy crow!* I thought startled. The manifested cup fell from my hands and crashed into the floor disappearing.

Learning that I could manifest was amazing. All silly thoughts of moving the cup were forgotten. I was sure that I could manifest something else if I tried. That gave me an idea. I was dying to be rid of my dirty clothes, so to start, I simply imagined my spirit self in fresh clothes instead of the tattered white dress that I last wore. It worked! Instantly I was in my favorite blue pajamas.

Feeling more comfortable, I tried to travel. Making it easy on myself, I pictured someplace familiar in my head, the rooftop garden at

Stryker. Just like in the bathroom, I was instantly where I wanted to be in the garden. Happy with my successes for the day, I stayed there for the afternoon.

When the evening came, I found myself back at the loft. Bow was already home. He looked terrible. I silently watched as he bathed, and climbed into bed beside my body. It was amazing how it had been two days, and my still form was just as perfect, and just as lovely as the day Temperance laid me to rest.

Bow looked better the next morning. He had some color in his cheeks. I wish he would eat something though. I watched him curiously as he sat on the couch in his gray sweat pants starring at the blank television screen. The coffee in his hand grew cold. I wondered where his mind was. I had lost my ability to openly hear his thoughts.

I grew bored watching him and wondering, so I occupied myself by manifesting. It was almost like playing dress up. I could envision any outfit, and instantly I was wearing it. I stood before the mirrored closet doors in Bows bedroom and posed.

First, I wore a prom dress and pretended to be awarded prom queen. When that grew tiresome, I traded the sparkly dress for a more sophisticated royal gown complete with a tiara and scepter. I blew fake kisses to my loyal subjects, and bowed before the mirror. That get-up eventually became dull too.

Next, I was covered in expensive jewels and designer apparel. I pretended to be rich and famous dodging the photographers as they tried to capture a picture of me. After a while, I grew tired of that game also. No matter how much of a distraction it was, I was still lost, and lonely.

I settled on wearing a comfy pink tunic and white stretch pants before I manifested a puzzle that I could do. I knew I could leave again and travel anywhere my heart desired if I wanted to, but somehow I couldn't bring myself to leave Bow when he appeared to be so vulnerable.

There was a timid knock on the door. It startled me. At first I didn't think Bow would answer it, but he eventually made his way to the door and opened it. Of course it was Temperance. She quickly swept into the loft looking more like an Angel than I had ever seen.

It had been a few days since I saw her. My last memory was not pleasant. The mascara-streaked face torn from sadness seemed to be gone now; a smile took its place. Temperance wore white slacks with a white blouse that was offset by a gold belt. Her hair was in an elegant twist leaving her beauty unmatched.

"She wouldn't want you to live like this, Buer. You need to eat something."

"I'm not hungry," he replied listless, taking a sip of his now cold coffee.

"Too bad. Do you think Amitiel risked her life saving you so that you could waste away like this in sadness?" She scolded. In a lighter tone she added, "I brought you a fresh bagel, please eat it."

Her smile was soft. She brought the food over to the couch where he had sat back down. She shoved aside crumpled newspapers and sat beside him placing the bagel in his hand. His eyes remained fixed on the television screen, but he did venture to take a couple of bites.

"What are you thinking about?" She asked.

"Ami. Always Ami." He had a sorrowful expression when he spoke my name.

"What about her?"

"I'm worried. I know she's caught between worlds. It scares me, I can't feel her presence anymore. Sometimes I tell myself she's here with me, but then I remind myself that it's impossible."

"Is it?"

I deserted my puzzle and was instantly by his side. He needed to know I was okay. I wasn't sure if this would work, but I closed my eyes and silently sent, 'I'm here.'

Bows head popped up and his eyes bugged out. I caught him off guard. It worked though. He got my message loud and clear.

Plans

I spent the last twenty-one hours conversing with Bow telepathically. I tried to persuade him to sleep, reminding him that I wasn't going anywhere, but he vehemently refused. I knew he was scared that if he closed his eyes, when he woke up I'd be gone. I did my best to comfort him by telepathically sending him peonies with the message, 'I only want to be with you.'

It was after nine in the morning, and Bow needed to go to work. It seemed to make leaving harder when he knew I was somewhere close. He gently kissed my still form as he always did, and left promising to return to me soon.

I found myself jaded in his absence. It felt nice to speak with him, and actually be heard. We had discussed what happened. I refused to let him take responsibility for my predicament. I made sure I was clear on the fact that his guilt was not necessary.

With the new day, and nothing but time, I decided to flex my new powers. Manifesting some white tennis shoes to walk in, I traveled to the pier where Bow and I kissed.

Summer was over now, and with the change in weather, the pier was close to deserted. There were a few fishermen bundled up in coats drinking whisky way too early, but otherwise I was alone. The cold no longer affected me. I couldn't feel any longer. That thought disturbed me.

My mind was restless. I drifted up and down the pier in a trance-like state. I passed by a Mother pushing her child in a stroller. I stopped to admire how happy they looked. Just then, the child looked at me with a puzzled expression.

I was shocked. No one had looked at me all day. They had looked through me, yes, but at me, no. Not until that moment. I ventured to speak, "Can you see me?" I asked the child out loud.

The child, far too young to answer my question, just giggled at me and reached for my face. I was astonished. In that moment, I knew where I was, and that there was surly hope!

I quickly returned to the loft hoping to find Bow, and tell him what I'd learned. I pretty much had the concept of traveling down. The more I did it, the easier it became. I was disappointed to find he wasn't there yet. I didn't want to miss him incase he was headed home, so I manifested my familiar blue pajamas, and decided to hang out.

Bow returned to me, as promised, an hour later. I bombarded his mind with telepathic messages the moment he was through the door. I filled him in on my adventure, and discovery.

"So you're sure the child saw you?" He asked excitedly.

'Yes, I'm sure. The child reached for my face.' I sent back.

"I never, in all of my years, knew that our kind was capable of falling into the lost realm."

'It is the only explanation.'

The lost realm is a world between worlds. It is a plane where souls go before moving on. It gives them the chance for final business, and goodbyes. If I was correct, and that truly is where I am, I know I can find a way back to my body.

†

Bow was up quite late last night with me, so I decided to let him sleep in. It was already past eleven, but I didn't have the heart to wake him. I heard Temperance at the door. It was awful not being able to touch objects. I wanted badly to open the door before she woke Bow. Instead, I sent her a message, 'he's asleep, come in.'

The knob turned and Temperance entered the loft bright eyed. "Good afternoon, Amitiel," she whispered looking around the room in search of me.

'I'm right in front of you,' I sent back laughing.

Her eyes became wide, and then she let out a peal of hushed laughter. "I kept hoping I'd see something. I must look silly."

I love Temperance. Her mere presence makes me happy.

'I can travel now. I need you to help me find the Fallen.'

"You can travel anywhere?" She asked astonished.

I watched her continuously look around the room. I knew she was hoping she'd be the one to catch a glimpse of my spirit. She crept over to the dining table and took a seat.

I took a moment to think before I answered. I really hadn't ventured any place that I wasn't familiar with, but I felt confident that it didn't matter. 'Yes, I believe I can. I cannot let this stop me. Where do you think I should look first?'

She jumped, placing her hand over her pounding heart. "I keep thinking I'll get used to hearing you in my head, Amitiel, but you startle me every time," she whispered. "Honestly, I'm not sure how to find them. I can recognize them, but not locate. My abilities are not as strong as yours are… or were."

"She's right, love. Only you can locate them," Bow interjected startling us both. He rolled off the couch and stretched. “Good morning.”

He yawned and rubbed his eyes. My gaze lingered. There was no sight like that of his sculpted bare chest. I wanted badly to reach out and stroke it. The desire to be whole again was so strong my heart ached.

“Good morning, Bow. Ami let me in,” Temperance said with a smirk.

Bows eyes popped open, and his eyebrows shot up in disbelief.

‘I merely told her to come in instead of knocking. I didn’t want her to wake you.’ My message was tinged with sadness that I couldn’t mask.

Bows face was instantly sullen. He knew I was unhappy.

Temperance, Bow, and I discussed my situation for what seemed like forever. In the end we decided that I had to be the one to find the Fallen. Bow was even optimistic that it was going to be easier with me being celestial, and all. I could travel quickly, and access any ones mind. Those had to be advantages.

Temperance was pretty confident that I could find the Fallen simply by wishing it so, just like with envisioning a certain place to travel to. I had to admit that she had me feeling confident.

The last problem I had was figuring out how to redeem them once they were found. No one seemed to have a clue. I offered that I could try to do as Lucifer did, and tap their foreheads, but neither Temperance nor Bow found that credible. Bow had the idea that I should say something. I mocked him by using an old man voice and saying, *'I release you"* in his head. For once, he actually laughed.

"I think you're on to something, Bow. Often when one confesses their sins, the Priest has to acknowledge them and offer forgiveness. Should it not be the same?" Temperance asked.

"I agree." Bow grabbed his Bible and started thumbing through it. As he was searching the pages, an old piece of paper fell from the tattered, well worn pages to the floor.

"This is it!" Bow exclaimed as he picked it up. "I'm sure of it."

The piece of old parchment read:

Prayer of St. Francis
Lord make me an instrument of your peace;
Where there is hatred, let me sow peace;
Where there is injury, pardon;
Where there is doubt, faith;
Where there is despair, hope;
Where there is darkness, light;
And where there is sadness, joy.

Grant that I may not so much seek to be consoled as to console;
To be understood as to understand;

To be loved as to love;
For it is in giving that we receive;
It is in pardoning that we are pardoned;
And it is in dying that we are born again in eternal life.

Redemption

I have been lost between worlds now for almost a full week. That roughly translates into one hundred and sixty-eight hours of being invisible. I could break it down into minutes, but it only gets more depressing.

I've been disillusioned way too long now. I have work to do regardless of my *situation.* Temperance and Bow have been a huge help. I now had a plan, and it was time to execute.

"What if you get lost?" Bow questioned. His worry for me was thick and apparent in the gray of his aura.

'I can't be certain, but I think if I concentrated hard enough on you, I'd be brought back,' I sent, trying to comfort him.

Temperance had work at the hospital today. She left late last night as it was. We spent several hours going over the St. Francis Prayer. She said that I had to memorize it word for word if our plan was to work.

Bow paced nervously. It seemed impossible to calm his fears. Every few minutes or so Bow tried to talk me out of going.

"I'm sure we can figure out a way to bring you back to your body where you belong, love. This journey can wait," he tried gently to persuade me.

'I'm going nuts here. I'm a ghost. You hold vigil over my lifeless body while I stand right next to you. Only you can't see. You have no idea how this feels!'

"No, I don't know. I do know that this is all my fault regardless of what you say." He pouted.

It was hard to remain angry. His pouting made me realize that this must be hard for him too.

'Well it sucks, okay? I am growing more and more restless by the minute. I'm tired of hanging around. I have work to do. I wish I could take you, but I can't. I'm trying really hard not to dwell on how hard it is going to be to leave you. Can you please just support me?' I argued telepathically.

After my mental research, upon Temperance's idea, I found that I could locate the Fallen. I found approximately two hundred. It will be quite a feat to accomplish. Finding them is only half of the battle. They have to *want* to be saved. I must not disregard their free will.

My plan was to travel to Hell first. I know Lucifer said he would not make them leave, and after thinking about it, I have to admit he was right. They chose to be there. Whether it is a poor decision or not, it is not my business. My only job now, is going to be finding them, and offering my hand in their redemption.

I hadn't really thought much about it, but I suppose some might refuse me. I mean, I even had a hard time wanting to leave Hell and return myself. Most fell for a reason. I guess I'll just have to cross that bridge if or when the time comes.

"I'm sorry," Bow finally said. "I'm going to be late for work." He began to tidy up the loft, putting laundry in the basket, dishes in the sink, and trash in the can.

I watched him meticulously move from room to room in a wasted effort to distract himself. I could tell from his aura he still harbored worry and regret.

Silently I sent, 'I'm sorry too.'

I didn't get a response this time. He purposefully chose to ignore me. He crossed the room, caressed my lifeless cheek, and whispered 'I love you' to my sleeping body, before he left.

What a punch in the gut. Hurt deeply, I quietly sent, 'Where ripples meet riptides, you'll find my love.' I disappeared from the loft, and set out on my journey.

I arrived in Hell a moment later. The trip was so much easier this time. There was no need to depend on snatchers. I simply thought of where

I wanted to be, closed my eyes, and opened them in Lucifer's office in the tower.

I watched Luc silently. He was reading a newspaper on the couch. There were so many things I wanted to tell him, but he looked so relaxed. I noted the clear blue skies outside the windows, and the soft breeze blowing through the palm trees. He must be in a good mood.

Right when I was going to suck it up, and send him a message, he spoke to me.

"I know you're here, Amitiel. Please stop fretting. I've been waiting for you."

Completely taken back, I telepathically responded, 'How did you know, Luc? My soul is lost.'

"I could sense your presence. Now tell me, what did you do to end up between worlds?" He asked sounding bored. He didn't even bother to look up from the paper.

'I healed Buer in order to save him.'

"That bloody bastard let you endanger yourself?" He asked outraged.

'Back up,' I crossed my arms in anger and stood invisible before him. 'What do you mean, let me? It was my duty. I could not let him die!' I returned equally as outraged.

"If I didn't love you, perhaps I would find myself cross over your stupidity."

'What you call stupidity, I call bravery.'

"You would." Despite himself Luc chuckled. "What can I do to help you," he asked finally setting the damn paper down.

'I've come to offer you my hand in redemption.'

Lucifer sat in silence. He was deep in thought. At one time, I would have felt guilty about eavesdropping in on someone's thoughts, now I wished for just the opportunity again.

"I am at a loss, my dear. I cannot go back. I rather enjoy the world I've created," he said with a smirk.

'Hell is quite the masterpiece,' I agreed. 'Though it is a shame you're not ready. As for the others, I'm sure you've sent word.'

"Indeed. Quite a few expect you."

'I'll be on my way then.' Before I took leave, I drifted back to Luc and hovered before him. I saw him shiver, so I knew he could sense me. Softly I kissed my dear friend on the cheek, and sent one last whispered message, 'Degas once asked, *Aren't all beautiful things made by renunciation?*'' With a gentle laugh, I disappeared.

I scoured Hell's depths to reach the Fallen. I am only now beginning to realize that Hell is what you make of it. Not all the places I have been were so elegant and beautiful. In fact, many were just the opposite.

In the countless hours that I have searched, I've ventured to a run down tavern where I saved five lost souls, an abandoned warehouse with ten more, a dreary old dock with an entire crew of twenty-three, even an alley that reeked of pee for four more. I did this all to save the Fallen.

It took weeks, but I eventually had racked up a total of one hundred and seventy nine Fallen Angels. All of which graciously accepted salvation. Each occasion I recited the St. Francis Prayer from memory as time around us stood still, and each time I stood back in awe as their wings returned. I then watched as they shimmered brightly and departed to Heaven happily.

I wanted badly to return to Bow. I wanted to tell him how well things were going, and that I loved and missed him terribly. I had a morose curiosity to see if my sleeping body still remained unchanged. In my heart, I knew it was not time to return yet.

I secretly hoped that with each soul saved I was closer to returning to my body. I had to keep the faith that God had a plan for me. I rationalized by thinking that with the tragic loss of my shell, I could do my work now without all my human frailties.

Soon I found myself back on earth, and in Paris. I had always wanted to visit there. I dreamt of finding inspiration, and painting on the knolls before the Eiffel Tower. That dream seems so silly now.

I stood beside a young florist peddling roses beneath the Arc de Triomphe. She instantly felt my presence.

"You've come," she spoke aloud to me.

'It is time,' I replied silently to her. 'Are you ready?'

"I've been ready and waiting for a long time," she said smiling up at the sky.

At that moment I knew she had accepted my help in salvation. I stood before her stopping time and recited the Prayer, 'Lord make me an instrument of your peace; where there is hatred let me sow peace; where there is injury, pardon; where there is doubt, faith; where there is despair, hope; where there is darkness, light; and where there is sadness, joy. Grant that I may not so much seek to be consoled as to console; to be understood as to understand; to be loved as to love; for it is in giving that we receive; it is in pardoning that we are pardoned; and it is in dying that we are born again in eternal life.'

The last phrase uttered set her free. She hurled forward and gasped in a brief moment of pain as her wings exploded from her back. I watched her smile and laugh, countless years of loss dissolved into love and peace in that moment.

Before departing, she acknowledged my presence and said, "Thank you."

There was no time, and no need for my welcoming return, as she was gone in a breathtaking shimmer. Time around me resumed. The only thing left to signify the Fallen Angel's existence on earth was the deserted rose cart before me.

Closing my eyes and following my heart, I opened my eyes again in Venice. I stood beside an architect sketching. He was seated at a small café in the Piazza San Marco.

'It's time,' I spoke silently to him.

He nodded and set his pencil down. No words were needed. He was ready. I stood before him stopping time and recited the Prayer, 'Lord make me an instrument of your peace; where there is hatred let me sow peace; where there is injury, pardon; where there is doubt, faith; where there is despair, hope; where there is darkness, light; and where there is sadness, joy. Grant that I may not so much seek to be consoled as to console; to be understood as to understand; to be loved as to love; for it is in giving that we receive; it is in pardoning that we are pardoned; and it is in dying that we are born again in eternal life.'

Moments later he was gone, and time resumed. The only thing left to signify the Fallen Angel's existence on earth was his abandoned sketch on the café table that trembled in the wind.

Once again closing my eyes and following my heart, I opened my eyes in Prague. I found myself standing beside a painter on the Charles

Bridge. He was deep in thought, doing his best to capture the essence of the Prague Castle before us. Sounds of boat engines could be heard form the Vltava River below. It was peaceful.

Once acknowledged, he too accepted my hand in his salvation. I stood before him stopping time and recited the Prayer tirelessly yet again, 'Lord make me an instrument of your peace… and it is in dying that we are born again in eternal life.'

He bent forward as if expecting what came next. His wings returned silently, but with great triumph. He flexed them in pleasure.

"I am forever in your debt," he said with a nod of his head. Moments later he was gone, and time resumed.

The only thing left to signify the Fallen Angels existence on earth was his half finished painting on the easel facing the Castle.

I could sense that my work would soon be complete. Most of the Fallen accepted salvation gladly. Only few were determined to stay. When I could not persuade them to return, I blessed them with my acceptance acknowledging their free will.

I found my self in a small cottage in Quebec next. It was snowing outside. The gable roof would certainly collapse if another storm hit. I stood beside an elderly man in a rocking chair before the stone hearth. For once I found myself thankful that I no longer could feel, for the gentleman looked cold.

"I heard whispers the key had come." His voice was haggard with age.

'It is time, kind Sir. I've come to pardon your sins. Heaven waits.'

"Heaven," he said with a smile. "I've long waited."

He was ready. I stood before him stopping time and recited the Prayer.

Everything was routine up until his wings returned. The once elderly man was young again. The countless years on earth that aged him had been erased, returning him to his former glory.

I stood there and wept, for this was a sight to be seen. His Angelic body was young, handsome, and strong once again. He nodded in my direction, and departed quickly. The only thing left to signify the Fallen Angel's existence on earth was the smoldering fire that remained the stone hearth.

Upon his exit, I instantly felt alarmed. Something was wrong. Where I could no longer feel, I now felt. First the cold draft through the rubble-stone wall of the cottage, then the splitting headache, followed by exhaustion. This wasn't right, I should have felt happy and strengthened by having saved yet another soul, but somehow the elderly man weakened me or so I thought.

I manifested a thick coat, and without thinking twice, I headed back to the loft, to Bows side for answers.

†

Bow could no longer stand my absence. When I entered, I found him knelt beside my sleeping body. To my shock and surprise, my shell remained unchanged. He was angry. He was yelling at my lifeless body.

"You promised me you'd be safe!" He screamed in my face. "I can't take this for another moment!" He was running out of steam. Deep shutters rocked his body as he cried in frustration.

I had never seen him so angry before. His aura was flaring a fiery red. It scared me. I watched as he moved from my side to the mantle, so I followed. I wanted to speak to him, but he needed to calm down. Bow reached for the one and only picture he had framed, and threw it with such force that it shattered on the floor.

He needed me. I needed to be whole again. 'ENOUGH!' I yelled at him telepathically.

Bow froze, "Amitiel?" He questioned in disbelief. His eyes flashed to my body, mistaking my mental message for the return of my soul. How I wished it were true.

I wanted nothing more that to feel his unshaven face on my cheek. To cover him in kisses, and reassure him that everything would be fine. It is said how love hurts, but this feeling was so intense I swear it would kill me.

"Amitiel, are you here? Have you returned?" Hope colored his aura.

I wanted to answer him. I tried, but I felt myself being pulled. The pull became so strong I had no choice but to stop resisting and follow. It led me right back into my sleeping body.

I had gotten my wish. I was whole again.

Ami and Buer's journey concludes in *Fate*

AVAILABLE NOW

www.ingramcontent.com/pod-product-compliance
Lightning Source LLC
La Vergne TN
LVHW010841120826
845149LV00020B/3453

* 9 7 8 0 9 8 9 0 0 3 3 7 7 *